Enid Blyton

Snowball the Pony

Text illustrations by Jan Lewis
Cover illustration by Alan Fredman

AWARD PUBLICATIONS LIMITED

Enid Blyton's Happy Days!

Snowball the Pony

Bimbo and Topsy

Run-About's Holiday

The Adventures of Binkle and Flip

Binkle and Flip Misbehave

Mister Meddle's Mischief

Mister Meddle's Muddles

Merry Mister Meddle

You're a Nuisance Mister Meddle

Collect all the titles in the series!

The Adventures of
Mr Pink-Whistle

Mr Pink-Whistle
Has Some Fun

Mr Pink-Whistle's
Party

Mr Pink-Whistle
Interferes

Hello
Mr Twiddle!

Mr Twiddle
in Trouble Again

Don't Be Silly,
Mr Twiddle!

Well, Really,
Mr Twiddle!

Shuffle
the Shoemaker

For further information on Enid Blyton please visit *www.blyton.com*

ISBN 978-1-84135-651-8

Illustrations copyright © Award Publications Limited

First published 1953 by Lutterworth Press

First published by Award Publications Limited 2004
This edition first published 2010

Published by Award Publications Limited,
The Old Riding School, The Welbeck Estate,
Worksop, Nottinghamshire, S80 3LR

11 2

Printed in the United Kingdom

Contents

Chapter 1
The Little Black Pony

A tiny pony stood by his mother in the corner of a field. He was so small that he wasn't much bigger than a big dog.

He had no name yet. The farmer he belonged to meant to sell him, so he hadn't bothered to give him a name.

He was black all over, as black as soot, and he had a nice long tail that he could whisk about, and bright eyes that noticed everything. His coat was like black satin, and his nose was as soft as velvet.

He was beautiful, and every child who saw him loved him and wanted him, but he was a wild little thing and wouldn't go near any boy or girl who called to him.

He loved his mother, and she loved him.

She often rubbed him softly with her nose, and he stood close to her to feel her warm, soft body. They lived in a big field together, and often liked to gallop round it.

'Have you lived here a long time, Mother?' said the little pony one day. 'All your life long?'

'Not all my life long,' said his mother. 'Most of it. I came here when I was very, very small, as small as you. I was given to the little boy, and I was his pony. He rode me for a long time, but now he is almost grown-up.'

'Who will ride *me*?' said the little pony, looking at his mother with big bright eyes.

'I don't know,' said his mother. 'There are no children here. The farmer may sell you, and you may go far, far away.'

'I don't want to,' said the little pony, and he pressed closely against his mother. 'I want to stay with you in this lovely sunny field always and always.'

'You won't be able to do that,' said his mother. 'It wouldn't be good for you. You must learn many things; you must go out into the big world; you must have a master; and you must grow up into a fine pony, loyal and obedient.'

'I don't want to,' said the tiny pony, in alarm. 'I should be afraid to leave you. Don't let me go away, Mother!'

'Well, you won't go yet,' said his mother. 'You are too small. Now let's go for a canter round the field and see if we can find where the grass grows long and juicy in the ditch.'

So they cantered off together, the little pony keeping close to his mother's side. They found the grass and nibbled it in delight. It was much nicer than the short grass in the field.

The farmer came to look at the tiny black pony a few days afterwards. His wife was with him.

'How lovely he is!' she cried. 'He looks like a toy pony! I wish we could keep him.'

'No, we must sell him,' said the farmer. 'He will bring joy to some child, who will ride him and love him. What a dear little fellow he is! I shall sell him next summer, but I will choose someone kind for him. He shall not go to any spoilt child who might whip him.'

'There! Did you hear that? You will soon be sold,' said the pony's mother. 'I shall miss you. But it will be nice for you to have your own home and a little master to love. The best thing in the world is to love and be loved, little pony, so be kind to everyone and make as many friends as you can.'

The little pony grew well in the next few months. How his black coat shone! There was nothing white about him at all except for a few hairs in his tail, and nobody ever noticed those.

'I expect you will be called Sooty or Blackie or Cinders,' said his mother. 'You are so very black.'

Soon the time came for him to be sold. He was to go the very next day. He was sad and kept close to his mother.

'Now don't worry,' she said to him. 'You will be quite all right. Always obey your master; always be kind; and take great care of any children who ride you.'

'Shan't I ever see you again?' said the little pony, sadly. 'I shall miss you so much.'

'Well, you are not going very far away,' said his mother. 'You are going to the children who live on the next farm to ours. So, perhaps some day you will be able to come over and see me. Maybe the children will ride you over here.'

'Oh, that will be lovely,' said the little pony. He began to feel excited. He was going out into the big world. How big was it? He didn't know, because he had never been out of the field-gate. He thought the world might be as far as the hills he could see.

The next day the farmer came, and, after giving the pony some oats, slipped a halter on to lead him away. He nuzzled against his mother for the last time and she rubbed him gently with her nose.

'Be good; be kind; do as you are told,' she

said. 'Then you will be happy. Goodbye, little pony.'

'Goodbye,' said the pony, and trotted out of the gate very sadly. It swung to and closed with a click. Now, for the first time, he was on the other side of the gate. The lane stretched out before him, looking very long.

The world seemed very big and very strange.

'Come along,' said the farmer. 'We are going to your new home.'

And off they went, the little pony looking round him with big, astonished eyes.

Chapter 2

A New Home
and a New Name

The little pony was surprised to find how big the world was. The lane was a long one and led into a main road, which seemed enormous to the little creature.

He jogged along by the farmer, looking in astonishment at the houses they passed. He had only seen the farmhouse before far away in the distance. Then suddenly a great red animal roared by, and the tiny pony leapt in fright, trying to jump into the ditch to hide.

'What's that?' he thought. 'Will it eat me, oh will it eat me?'

'Now, now,' said the farmer, laughing, 'that was only a bus. It won't hurt you! Come along.'

Soon they left the main road and went into another lane. This led over the blue hills that the pony had so often seen from his field. He saw cornfields on each side, growing green, with a poppy or two flashing a red eye at him now and again.

They came to the top of the hill and the pony looked in surprise at the valley below. Why, the world was even bigger than he had thought! It was an enormous place!

'Now, there's your new home, down there,' said the farmer, and he nodded at a pretty farmhouse nestling down in the valley. 'You'll like living there. There are three children to ride you, and they're nice children, so don't you try any silly tricks with them.'

The pony pricked up his ears. Three children! He would like that. He was shy of boys and girls, but once he knew them it would be great fun to play with them. He jogged on happily, feeling more and more excited.

They came to the farm. A little white gate led to the farmhouse. Swinging on it were three children, waiting for them. They saw the tiny pony and shouted in delight.

'There he is! Look, there he comes! Oh, isn't he sweet? He's the nicest little pony we've ever seen!'

They jumped off the gate and rushed to meet the farmer and the pony. He was afraid and ran back, nearly pulling the rope from the farmer's hand. But the farmer pushed him forward.

'What, you're shy! Don't be silly! Just show how beautiful you are!'

'He *is* beautiful,' said Willie, a big boy of ten. 'The most beautiful pony I've ever seen.'

'Oh the darling!' said Sheila, who was seven, and she put her arms round his neck.

'I want to ride him now, now, now!' cried Timmy, the youngest. He was five. The farmer lifted him up and put him on the pony's back, holding him there. The pony jumped in fright. He was not used to having anyone on his back, and he didn't like it.

'Now, now!' said the farmer. 'You'll have to get used to this. Well, Timmy, how do you like him?'

'I love him,' said Timmy, his round face red with joy. 'Take me off again. I want to look at him.'

'Well, I must leave him now,' said the farmer. 'Where's he to be kept?'

'In the field just here,' said Willie, and he pointed to the field near the farmhouse garden. 'I'll take him. Oh, isn't he lovely? Has he got a name?'

'No,' said the farmer, giving the rope to Willie to lead the pony away. 'I left it to you children to name him. Well, I hope he'll be good. He's a dear little fellow. Now I'll go and have a word with your father. I can see him in the fields up above.'

He left the pony with the children. They led him into the field and shut the gate. He stood and looked at them with his bright, puzzled eyes. Everything was so strange to him. He wanted his mother there.

'You're the dearest pony in the world, and you're ours!' said Sheila, rubbing his nose gently. 'But first we must give you a name.'

'*Not* Sooty or Blackie or Cinders,' said Willie.

'But he's *very* black!' said Sheila. 'We ought to call him something black.'

'I don't like black names,' said Willie. 'I shan't call him a black name.'

'Oh well, call him Snowball or Snow-white

or Snowdrop!' said Sheila, laughing. The others stared and Willie laughed too.

'Good idea! We'll call him Snowball! That will make people laugh. Anyway, it's a nice name. Snowball, do you like your new name?'

The pony turned his head to Willie. He liked Willie. He didn't know what a snowball was. He had never seen snow. He thought it was a nice name, and he was very glad to have a name of his own. He hoped his mother would like it too.

'Snowball!' said Sheila, softly, in his ear. 'That's your name, little pony. Snowball! Now, when you hear us calling that, you must always come trotting over to us. See?'

'Snowball,' said Timmy, and he patted the pony on the neck. 'You're a black snowball, and you're ours and we love you.'

'We won't try to ride him today,' said Willie. 'He's shy and frightened because he's been brought away from his home. We'll just talk to him and trot him about. He'll soon settle down and be happy!'

'Come along, Snowball, come round the field,' said Sheila.

And Snowball trotted off with the three children in delight.

Chapter 3
Snowball's Field

Soon the children went in to their dinner, and their mother heard all about Snowball. She promised to go out and see him afterwards.

'He will be a lovely pet for you,' she said, 'and even Timmy will be able to ride him. I think Daddy is bringing tack for him today, because soon he will have to learn how to carry a saddle, and obey the reins.'

'He won't like that at first,' said Willie. 'But he will soon get used to it. He's so sweet, Mother. I've never seen such a lovely pony. His coat is like gleaming black satin.'

'Whatever made you call him Snowball?' said his mother, smiling. 'That's a good joke!'

'I hope he's not feeling very lonely in the field by himself,' said Sheila. 'I expect he's missing his mother very much.'

Snowball was feeling very lonely. He wanted the children to come and talk to him again. Where had they gone and when would they come back?

He nibbled some grass and it tasted rather nice. He wandered round the field, and felt proud to think it was *his* field. There was no other creature in it. There were cows in the next field, and sheep on the hill side. But he was the only creature in his own field.

But what was this? A brown hen came through the hedge and began to peck at the ground in his field. Then another hen came and another. Snowball stood and looked at them angrily.

'This is *my* field!' he neighed to them and he ran up fiercely. The first brown hen looked surprised.

'*Your* field? What do you mean? We always come in here to peck about. Don't be silly.'

'Go away,' said Snowball. 'I won't have you here!' He ran at the hen and she scuttled back into the hedge. Then he ran at the other two, and they went off as well. But no sooner had he turned his back than the first hen came back again through another hole further off.

Snowball was cross. He trotted over to the hen and she gave a cluck and ran off – but just as she went into the hedge some more hens came in at the opposite side of the field. Snowball galloped across to tell them what he thought of them.

Soon the hens were having a fine game with the little pony. 'Can't catch *me*! Can't catch *me*!' first one hen clucked and then another. Snowball dashed at them all, and then he stamped his hoof.

'I shall tell the children! You know this is my field, and I don't allow anyone else in it.'

A big brown horse looked over the hedge, and stared at Snowball. 'Hello!' he said. 'I haven't seen you before. What's all this fuss about?'

'It's these hens,' said Snowball. 'It's the first time I've had a field of my own, and I don't want hens in it.'

'This isn't your field,' said the big brown horse. 'It's only the field where you are allowed to be. As for the hens, they can go anywhere. The farmer said so. Don't be

unkind, or you will make no friends. Didn't your mother tell you that?'

Snowball suddenly thought of his mother. Yes, she *had* told him that. Oh dear – and he had forgotten so soon. What a pity! He hung his head down and trotted off to a corner. The hens came round and clucked at him.

'He's only a baby after all! He doesn't know any better. What's your name, baby?'

The pony felt glad he had a name. 'My name is Snowball,' he said.

Then the hens and the brown horse laughed loudly. 'What a joke!' they said to one another. 'Snowball! Think of that! What a black Snowball!'

The gate clicked and the pony heard the voices of the children. He pricked up his ears and looked round.

'Snowball! Snowball!' called the three children. The little pony galloped gladly over to them.

'He knows his name already!' cried Willie. 'Isn't he clever? He came as soon as he was called.'

The pony nuzzled against them. Timmy held something out to him, something square and white on the palm of his hand.

Snowball sniffed at it.

'Go on, Snowball, it's a treat for you. It's a piece of sugar,' said Timmy. 'Eat it, silly!'

Snowball sniffed again. He had never smelt sugar before. He suddenly lifted his upper lip and took the sugar lump into his mouth.

He crunched it. It was sweet and he liked it very much. He sniffed round Timmy hoping to find another bit of sugar. What a nice boy this was, to give him such a treat!

'I may bring you a lump of sugar tomorrow, if you're good,' said Sheila. 'Come

along. Let's see you gallop and trot and walk and roll. We've come to play with you for the whole afternoon!'

Soon the four of them were playing madly together, with all the hens looking on in surprise. The children galloped round the field and the pony galloped too. They walked and he walked. They lay down on the grass and he lay down too.

Then they rolled over and over and the pony rolled over as well. That was a game he liked! The children laughed.

'He's just like us!' said Timmy. 'He likes just the same things as we do!'

Chapter 4
Snowball and Sheila

The first night Snowball felt dreadfully lonely without his mother to snuggle up against. Usually she lay down beneath a big chestnut tree in her field, and the little pony cuddled close up to her.

But tonight, in his own field, there was no one to cuddle against. He neighed for his mother, but she didn't come. She was far away. He looked for the brown hens to talk to, but they had gone to bed in the hen-house.

He went to the hedge and neighed for the old brown horse. But the horse was asleep at the other end of the field and didn't come.

An owl came out and screeched suddenly. It made Snowball jump.

Then a hedgehog ran by, and scraped

against his hooves.

And then the moon rose up, a big round lamp in the sky, that seemed like a face to Snowball.

He was lonely and afraid. He stood under a tree and trembled. He was very unhappy. Nobody loved him. Everyone had forgotten about him! He wanted to run away, but the field-gate was shut.

But somebody remembered him. Somebody lay still in her warm bed, and thought of the little pony out in the field alone for the first time in his life. Somebody was sad for him, and wanted to comfort him.

That somebody was Sheila. Sheila loved her dolls and all her toys, and now she loved the pony.

She got up and went to the window. The moon was up and she could see the pony's field.

Then she saw him, standing up, quite still, in one corner. 'He's awake! He can't go to sleep. He wants his mother!' thought the little girl. 'Poor little Snowball. I'll pull on my dressing-gown and steal downstairs and run to the field. It's such a fine night I shan't get cold.'

She put on her dressing-gown, and crept down the stairs. She undid the front door and slipped out. She ran down the garden path to the white gate. Then she went to the field and opened the gate there.

Snowball heard the click and was alarmed. Who was this? Who could it be in the middle of the night? His mother had always told him that people who crept about at night-time were not good people. Had someone come to steal him?

He stood and shivered, as Sheila came through the gate. Then he heard a soft voice, 'Poor little Snowball! Are you lonely? I've just come to tell you not to be unhappy, and to give you a hug.'

Snowball knew Sheila's voice. His heart jumped for joy. He trotted over to her at once, nuzzling against her, almost knocking her over. He was delighted to see someone he knew. She put her arms round him, and he felt her heart beating against his nose. Nice girl! He would love her the best because she was so kind.

'Now you lie down here, under this tree where the ground is dry,' said Sheila, and she led him to a good place. 'You'll soon be asleep. Nothing will harm you here.'

Snowball took hold of her dressing-gown gently with his teeth. He pulled at it.

'What, you want me to lie down near you!' said Sheila. 'What a funny little pony you are! Do you miss your mother tonight! Well, I'll cuddle up to you for a little while, then I must go in.'

It was a very warm night. Snowball and

Sheila lay down on the dry grass, and Sheila put her head on the pony's round body. He was quite happy now. Somebody loved him, and was his friend. That was what his mother had said – he must get friends and he would be happy.

He fell asleep – and so did Sheila! The round moon looked down on them both. A hedgehog came up and stared at them in surprise.

They both slept for hours. Then Dan, the farm-hand, came into the field – and how surprised he was to see Sheila and Snowball asleep together under the tree!

'Hi, Missy!' he said, gently, and shook her shoulder. 'You'll get into trouble for sleeping out of doors. You might get a dreadful cold!'

Sheila woke up and stared into the green leaves of the tree above her. She saw the blue sky between some of the leaves.

Wherever could she be?

She sat up and saw Dan. 'Oh dear!' she said. 'I must have been out here all night! Whatever will Mother say? She will be very cross with me. I wonder if I can slip into the house without being seen.'

'No, don't you do that,' said Dan. 'You tell your mother, see? It doesn't do to hide things, that's not right. My, that's a fine little black pony, isn't it? What's his name?'

'Snowball,' said Sheila, and that made Dan laugh.

'What a joke!' he said. He stroked Snowball, and the pony pushed his nose against him. He nuzzled against Sheila too. He thought he would never, never forget how the little girl had come out to him on the night when he was so lonely. He would love Sheila best.

The little girl ran indoors. Her mother saw

her coming and was surprised. 'Surely you haven't been out in the fields in your dressing-gown!' she said.

'Oh Mother, I've been out all night, quite by mistake!' said Sheila. 'Snowball was so lonely, and I knew he was missing his mother. So I went out to him, and we cuddled up together. And I fell asleep and Dan woke me up. Don't be cross with me!'

Mother wasn't. She gave Sheila a kiss and said, 'You're always such a kind little girl, aren't you!'

After that, Sheila and Snowball were always special friends.

Chapter 5

Snowball Makes a Few Friends

Snowball soon settled down in his new home. He loved all the children. One or other of them always brought him a lump of sugar, and he looked forward to that.

Soon he was allowed to go wherever he wanted to. His gate was not always shut, and he wandered in and out as he liked. He was as much a pet as Tinker, the farm-dog.

Snowball liked his new home. He soon began to know all the other animals on the farm. He went round to tell them who he was.

He went into the field where the cows were. They stared at him, munching all the time. He looked at their horns and felt a little afraid.

'You won't toss me, will you?' he said. 'Promise you won't.'

'Of course not. We don't use our horns for tossing,' said Buttercup, a red and white cow. 'The *bull* might use his horns to toss you, though, so don't go near him.'

'I'm Snowball, the new Shetland pony, and I belong to the children,' said Snowball. The cows laughed.

'Snowball! What an odd name for you! We have never seen a horse as tiny as you are. We thought you were a toy one at first.'

'I'm not a toy! I'm alive!' said Snowball. 'See how fast I can gallop!'

He galloped round and round the field and the cows watched him. 'You gallop almost as fast as Captain, the big brown horse over there,' said Buttercup.

Snowball ran up to Captain. 'Hello!' he said. 'I'm Snowball, the Shetland pony. I can gallop faster than you, I'm sure.'

'Ah, you're the fellow who played "catch" with the hens and couldn't catch them, aren't you?' said Captain, with a twinkle in his eye. 'Well, I'll run a race with you if you like.'

So they ran a race round and round the

field, but Captain won. He was a strong and powerful horse, and though Snowball galloped as fast as he could, he couldn't keep up with Captain.

'I can't gallop as fast as you can, after all,' said Snowball, panting.

'No. It's better not to boast of what you can do, till you've tried,' said Captain. 'Now, where are you off to?'

'I'm going to talk to those round pink creatures over there,' said Snowball. 'What are they? They make such a funny grunting noise.'

'Pigs,' said Captain. 'Now, don't you go into their sty, because if you do the old sow may come after you. She doesn't like people she doesn't know.'

But Snowball took no notice. He trotted off to the pigsty. He pushed against the gate. It didn't open. Then he remembered seeing one of the children press down the catch at one side of the gate. That made the gate open.

So with his nose he pressed on the catch. It opened. Aha, how clever he was! He trotted into the pigsty, and all the piglets ran round him in wonder.

'What are you? Who are you?'

'I'm Snowball, the Shetland pony, and I am allowed to go where I like,' said Snowball. 'Ah, what's in your trough? It smells good!'

He went over to the pig-trough, in which Dan had put pig-food. He began to nibble bits here and there.

The old mother sow, who had been lying down on her side, lifted her head and looked at him.

'What are you doing in here, eating our food?' she grunted. 'Go out at once. And shut the gate behind you. I don't want my piglets running all over the farm.'

Snowball ran to the gate and shut it. But he didn't go out of it first! No, he shut himself in, and went back to the trough to find another titbit.

The big old sow was angry. She stood herself up on her four short legs and looked crossly at Snowball out of her little piggy eyes.

'Bad pony!' she said. 'Stealing our food, and opening our gate! Bad pony!'

She ran at Snowball and almost knocked him over. He was frightened. She looked so very long and fat and big.

The piglets ran round him, squealing, 'Run away, silly, run away!'

So he ran round the pigsty with the old mother-pig lumbering after him. The piglets ran too, squealing in excitement, getting under his feet. Oh dear, why had he come into this horrid place?

Willie heard all the noise. He ran to the pigsty, and how he laughed.

'Mother, look! Sheila, look! Snowball has got in among the pigs, and the old sow is chasing him!'

Everyone laughed and Snowball was ashamed. Willie opened the pigsty and Snowball rushed out. The pigs put their pink noses through the lowest bars of the gate and squealed again.

'Come and see us again, Snowball. It's fun to see Mother chasing you!'

'Did you open the gate yourself?' said Willie to Snowball, astonished. 'My goodness, what a clever pony you are! But don't you go into the pigsty again. The old sow doesn't like it.'

'I won't,' neighed Snowball, and trotted back to his own field for a rest. 'Dear me, how glad I am that I didn't have a fierce mother like that old sow! I am sorry for all those piglets!'

Chapter 6
A Saddle and
Bridle for Snowball

The first time that Snowball had on a saddle and bridle he didn't like it at all. He couldn't understand what was on his back. He didn't like the bridle either, and he tossed his head up and down angrily.

'Now, don't be silly, Snowball,' said Sheila, in her gentle voice. 'We all want to ride you, and we can't if you don't have a saddle for us to sit on, and reins to guide you.'

She gave him a lump of sugar. He munched it and stood quietly. He looked at her out of the corners of his eyes. If Sheila wanted him to do something, he would do it. Yes, he would do anything for Sheila, even if he didn't like it.

'You get on first, Sheila,' said Willie. 'The pony loves you so much, ever since that night you spent with him in the field. He may stand quietly for you.'

So Sheila got on to his back. How heavy she felt at first. How uncomfortable! Snowball wanted to rear up and throw off this sudden weight.

But he couldn't bear to make Sheila fall off. She might be hurt. So he stood still, trembling.

'Dear Snowball, dear good Snowball,' said Sheila, and she stroked his thick black mane.

'Walk with me on your back, Snowball. You and I are one, now, can't you feel how we belong to one another, now that you carry me on your back? Our Daddy says that that is one of the nicest feelings between a man and a horse. Can't you feel it, Snowball?'

She pressed her legs against his sides. He

stopped trembling. He walked a few steps. He suddenly liked Sheila being on his back. He stopped and looked round at her. She patted him.

'Good boy,' she said. 'Clever boy! You will soon be as good to ride as Captain, the old brown horse.'

'I'm better than Captain for you, because I am the right size!' neighed Snowball, and he suddenly set off round the field, with Sheila holding the reins in delight. Bumpity-bumpity-bump! Bumpity-bumpity-bump! she went.

'Steady, Snowball, steady, you're bumping me so!' cried Sheila. 'This is your first lesson so you must only walk with me.'

So Snowball walked and jogged round the field with Sheila on his back. Sheila laughed for joy, and her cheeks went bright red. Her eyes shone.

'He's lovely to ride!' she called. 'Simply lovely. He will go like the wind! Whoa, Snowball. Whoa! When I pull the reins in like this, you must stop. That's right.'

Timmy had a ride next. He wasn't so good at riding as Sheila was, for she had often ridden before. So Willie went beside them, his hands on the reins.

Then Willie had his turn and he walked and trotted round the field. The noise of Snowball's little hooves made all the brown hens scuttle away into the hedge.

Snowball felt proud when at last Willie dismounted. He had taken three children for rides. He had got used to a saddle almost at once. He knew how to answer the pull of the reins.

'He's really very clever,' said Willie, and he patted Snowball's velvety nose. 'He'll do anything for us. He was frightened at first, but he soon got over it. Isn't he lovely to ride, Sheila?'

'Yes, lovely,' said Sheila. 'He's just the right size for us. Even if Timmy fell off his back it wouldn't matter, because he wouldn't have far to fall! Good boy, Snowball. We'll take you over to see your mother tomorrow, if you like, and show her how well you've got on. That shall be your reward for being so good.'

Snowball galloped round the field all by himself in delight. To see his mother! Oh, how lovely! And she would see how well he carried the children on his back, and he could tell her about the pigs and cows and everything.

So the next day the four of them, with

Tinker the farm-dog, started off to the near-by farm. Mother had said that as it was such a fine day they could take their lunch with them and have it in the fields.

They saddled Snowball. Then they set off, taking it in turns to ride on his back. He felt very proud, because everyone they met stared hard. Boys and girls ran up to them and patted Snowball. 'Oh, is he yours? Isn't he a beauty? What's his name?'

'Snowball,' said Willie, and the children laughed.

'What a funny name for a black pony! Can we have a ride?'

'Not today,' said Willie. 'He's only just learnt to have us on his back. We're taking him to see his mother.'

'Let me have a ride on him, do,' said a big boy, tugging at the reins.

'Let go,' said Willie. 'No, Lennie, you can't. You're too big, for one thing, and for another you're not kind to animals. Let go!'

'Well, I shall come and get him to ride one day when you're all out!' said Lennie, looking sulky. 'See? That's what I'll do if you don't give me a ride now.'

'Don't be silly,' said Willie. 'Come on, Sheila, you get on Snowball's back now. It's your turn.'

Sheila got up, and they went off again. Tinker followed them, looking round and growling at Lennie. Nobody liked Lennie. He was selfish and unkind.

'Here we are!' said Willie at last, as they came in sight of the farm. 'There's your old field, Snowball.'

'And there's my mother!' whinnied Snowball, in delight. 'Look, there she is!'

Chapter 7
A Visit to Snowball's Mother

With Sheila on his back the little pony trotted to the gate of the field he knew so well. He whinnied loudly. His mother lifted her head and saw him at the gate.

She galloped over at once, whinnying too. She and Snowball rubbed noses lovingly.

'We'll have our picnic in this field,' said Willie. 'Then Snowball and his mother can have a nice long time together.'

Sheila got off Snowball's back, took his saddle and bridle off and led him through the gate, which Willie had opened. The children followed and shut the gate. They found a nice place on a sunny bank and sat down to eat their lunch.

'Look at Snowball and his mother,' said Timmy. 'Aren't they pleased to see one another?'

Snowball looked round the field. He remembered how it had seemed enormous to him, like half the world. Now it looked very small! How strange. Had he grown, or had the field got small?

His mother looked smaller to him too. So he must have grown. His mother told him he had got bigger.

'You're almost as big as I am!' she said. 'How quickly you've grown! Have you got a name yet?'

'Yes. It's Snowball,' said the pony. His mother thought that was funny.

'Why is it funny?' asked Snowball. 'Everyone laughs at my name. Why do they?'

49

'Wait till next winter comes and you will know why,' said his mother. 'Now, tell me everything about your new home. Are the children nice?'

Snowball told her everything. He told her about how Sheila had come to comfort him on his first lonely night, and his mother was glad.

'She must be a dear little girl,' she said. 'I will let her ride me after she has had her lunch.'

'They're all nice,' said Snowball. 'Except the old sow, who looks after the piglets. She chased me.'

'Look, the children are calling us. They have got some oats,' said his mother. So they cantered over to the children.

When they had finished the oats, Sheila held out a young carrot for Snowball's mother, who took it eagerly. She loved carrots.

Snowball sniffed at it.

'Try one, Snowball,' said Willie. 'You'll like it.'

Snowball liked it very much and nosed in the lunch-bag for another. He found one and took it out.

'Oh look – Snowball is helping himself!' cried Sheila. 'No, Snowball, don't you take those apples! They're for us!'

But Sheila gave Snowball the apple cores and he crunched them up, pleased. Then he went round the old field with his mother, looking for the places he knew. Yes, there was the tree they used to sleep under. And there was the ditch where the long juicy grass grew. And there was the trough in which the farmer always put water, because there was no stream or pond in the field.

Soon the children got up and went over to the ponies. Snowball's mother tried to show Sheila that she would like to give her a ride. But she had no saddle.

'I think I could ride her bareback if she would let me hold her mane,' said Sheila, and got up on to the pony's back. Soon she was trotting round the field, and Timmy followed her on Snowball. Willie stood in the middle, waving a long twig about, pretending he was a circus ringmaster, and they were his circus ponies and riders!

'It's time to go home,' said Sheila at last, getting off the mother pony's back. 'Thank you, I loved that ride. Snowball, say goodbye

to your mother.'

'You won't be lonely again without me, will you?' said Snowball's mother, nuzzling against him. 'Do you want to stay here with me? Are you sad to go away?'

'No,' said Snowball. 'I love my new home, and I love the three children. I don't want to stay here, Mother. But I'll come and see you again soon, even if I have to come by myself. Goodbye!'

'Goodbye, Snowball!'

He walked away, with Timmy on his back, a sleek and shining pony. His mother watched him go, very proud of him. The gate clicked.

They were gone.

Chapter 8
Snowball Is Funny

Once, when the three children were all indoors, because it was pouring with rain, Snowball felt wet and cold and lonely.

He stood under a tree, but the rain was coming down so hard that he got wet even there. He whinnied crossly.

'I'm getting wet. I shall get a cold. My mother always told me not to get a chill. Even the hens are safely in their house – but I am left out in this field all by myself!'

He heard some ducks splashing in a big puddle on the other side of the hedge. He looked over and spoke to them.

'Fancy being out in the rain! How stupid you are! You will get wet through.'

'Ah, this is proper duck's weather,'

quacked a big drake. 'We love the rain. The wetter it is the more we like it. Our bodies never get wet. The rain slips off our feathers, you know.'

'The pigs are in their sty, the cat is in the house, the hens are underneath their wooden hut, the dog is in his kennel – but I am here getting wetter and wetter and wetter!' whinnied Snowball, feeling more and more sorry for himself.

'Well, go and ask the hens if you can shelter in their house,' said the ducks, splashing

hard. 'There is plenty of room there.'

So Snowball cantered to the gate of his field. It was shut, but he knew how to open any field-gate, clever little pony! Soon the gate was open and he trotted over to the big hen-house.

But the hens did not want him in there. 'No, no, you chased us out of your field the other day,' they said. 'We don't want you in our house.'

Then Snowball went to the kitchen door and looked in to see if the cat was there. She was lying on the mat by the kitchen fire.

'Can I come in and lie down by the fire too?' said Snowball.

'Good gracious, no!' said the cat. 'Only dogs and cats are allowed indoors. Go away.'

But Snowball went right into the kitchen, and was just going to lie down by the fire when the daily help came in. 'My goodness!' she cried in astonishment, 'Whatever next! Snowball, go out at once! Stamping all over the kitchen! Do you want to be smacked?'

Then Snowball went to Tinker's kennel. Tinker wasn't there. The kennel was made of an enormous old tub set on its side.

Inside was some straw. It looked very, very comfortable.

'This looks good,' thought Snowball. 'I'm so small, and the tub is so big, I believe I could get into it and lie down.'

So into the tub he got, pushing himself in backwards very carefully. He lay down in the straw. It was dry and soft and comfortable. Snowball was happy.

'I wish I was a dog. I wish I had a kennel like this. Tinker is very lucky,' he said to himself. And then he fell asleep.

The rain stopped. The sun came out. The children came out, too, and looked for Snowball, because they wanted to ride him.

'He's not in his field!' said Sheila, surprised. 'He's opened the gate and gone. Snowball! Where are you?'

There was no answer. Then suddenly, from the yard, came the sound of loud barking. It was Tinker.

'Whatever's the matter with Tinker?' said Timmy.

Tinker was standing outside his kennel, barking loudly. And there, inside, just waking up, was Snowball, looking very surprised.

'*Snowball!* Oh! do look, Snowball's put

himself in Tinker's kennel!' cried Willie, and how they all laughed.

Snowball scrambled out and shook himself. He neighed and trotted up to Sheila. He was glad to see her, and he put his nose into her hand.

'You're a funny darling pony!' said Sheila, and she laughed at him. 'I'm sure no other pony in all the world has slept in a dog's kennel, Snowball. Whatever will you think of next?'

Chapter 9
The Bad Boy, Lennie

Once Lennie came to see Willie, Sheila and Timmy. They didn't much want to see him, because they didn't like him. He was very unkind and selfish.

But Mother had always said they must be polite to visitors, so they were quite nice to him.

'I want to ride that pony of yours,' said Lennie.

'No, we'd rather you didn't,' said Sheila, very politely. 'He's still rather new, and although he's used to us, he might not like you riding him. You see, you are very fat and heavy.'

'Don't be rude,' said Lennie, frowning. He *was* very fat, because he was a greedy boy, but he didn't like being reminded of it, of course.

'I'm not being rude,' said Sheila, surprised. 'I'm just telling you why you can't ride Snowball.'

'Well, I'm going to,' said Lennie, who knew that the children's father and mother were out. He went over to Snowball's field. The children ran after him.

'You're not to, Lennie,' said Willie.

'You can't stop me,' said Lennie. 'I'm much bigger than you are. I could knock you all down with one hand.'

'You're a very horrid boy,' said Sheila, almost in tears.

Timmy caught hold of Lennie's coat and tried to drag him back. Lennie shook himself free and Timmy fell over.

Then Lennie ran fast to the field, climbed the gate and called to Snowball. 'Snowball, come here!'

'No, don't come, don't come!' cried Sheila.

But Snowball did come. He always came when he was called. He came now, trotting up, his bright eyes looking from one child to another, ready to give any of them a ride.

But it was Lennie who jumped on his back. Lennie had no saddle or bridle for the pony, but he didn't care. He held on to Snowball's thick black mane, and clasped him tightly with his strong knees.

'Gallop!' cried Lennie. 'Go on, gallop!'

Snowball didn't like this boy. He was fat and heavy, and he didn't feel nice. Lennie kicked hard against the pony's sides, and Snowball jumped in fright. He wasn't used to people being rough with him.

'Oh Lennie, don't! Oh Lennie, get off!' cried Sheila, running after them. But now Snowball was galloping in alarm over the field, bucking as he went, afraid of Lennie's hard heels.

'Here we go, here we go!' cried Lennie, enjoying himself. 'Go on, Snowball, faster, faster!'

Snowball didn't like this boy on his back. He was a horrid boy. The little pony suddenly stopped dead, and Lennie shot right over his head, and landed with a bump on the grass.

All the three children laughed. It served Lennie right. But Lennie was very angry indeed. He went to the hedge and cut a thick stick with his knife, holding on to Snowball all the time.

Then he jumped on to the pony's back again and began to hit him hard with the stick.

'I'll teach you to throw me over your head, you wicked pony!' he cried. The three children rushed up to stop him, but Lennie made Snowball gallop away from them.

Nobody knew what to do. Lennie was such a big boy. But Snowball knew what to do.

He wasn't going to put up with that boy one minute longer!

He galloped to the open gate. He galloped right through it. He galloped to the pond where the ducks were swimming lazily.

He galloped right to the very edge – and then, just as suddenly as before, he stopped – and over his head again went Lennie, straight into the muddy duck-pond!

The ducks fled in fright, quacking loudly. Snowball raised his head and neighed in delight. Sheila, Willie and Timmy roared with laughter. Lennie had got a very good punishment indeed.

The surprised boy went head-over-heels into the water. He struggled to his feet,

choking and spluttering, angry and frightened. He waded out, weeds hanging from his hair, his clothes dripping wet.

'What will my mother say?' he said, and, to Willie's astonishment, he began to howl loudly.

'Baby!' said Willie. 'You are bully enough to kick and whip a little pony, and baby enough to howl when you're punished! Go home. I won't tell my father about you this time, because Snowball himself has punished you.'

Lennie went home, still howling. Snowball stood with the three children, neighing.

'You're the cleverest pony I ever knew!' said Timmy, hugging him. 'We needn't worry about you, ever, because you always find a way out of any difficulty. Good little Snowball! Come and have a special lump of sugar.'

Chapter 10
Snowball Uses His Brains

Every week Willie rode on Snowball's back to the village, to fetch the papers for his father. There were five weekly papers; three for his father and two for his mother.

Snowball soon knew when Friday came. He didn't wait for Willie to come and fetch him. He opened the gate with his nose, and trotted down to the garden-door of the house. He knew Willie would come rushing out in a minute or two.

'Hello, Snowball!' Willie would shout. 'Always on time, aren't you! Come on, we'll go and get the papers. I've got the money.'

But one day, when Snowball went down to the garden-door and waited patiently, no

Willie came. Snowball stamped his feet and neighed. That meant 'Willie, come along,

you *are* late!'

But still no Willie came. Then the daily help shouted from the kitchen: 'My, there's Snowball waiting for Willie to fetch the papers as usual! He doesn't know Willie's in bed with a cold!'

Snowball pricked up his ears. What, Willie in bed! Oh, that was why he hadn't seen him all day, then.

Poor Willie!

Snowball trotted off. He stood in the lane, thinking. He knew the way to the village. He knew the paper shop. Why shouldn't he go by himself? The woman at the shop would know what he had come for.

The clever little pony set off by himself, tossing his head and whisking his long tail proudly. He was going to fetch the papers. He felt most important.

'I'm fetching the papers,' he told all the dogs he met.

'I'm fetching the papers,' he told the old cart-horses he passed. Everyone stared at him in wonder.

He came to the village. 'Oh look, there's

Willie's dear little Shetland pony out by him-self!' cried all the children, and Snowball whinnied to them too.

'I'm fetching the papers!'

He came to the paper shop. There was a bell-pull that hung outside the door. Snowball would have gone into the shop if the door had been open, but it wasn't. He had often seen Willie pull the bell, so he reached up to it with his mouth, took hold of the rope, and dragged it down.

'Ring-ting-ting!' the bell jangled loudly. Then Snowball knocked with his hoof on the ground. 'Knock, knock, knock,' just as he did when Willie was on his back, waiting to get the papers.

The shop-woman opened the shop door and looked out, expecting to see Willie. But only Snowball was there, and she stared in surprise.

'Why, where's Willie?' she said. 'Have you come without him?'

Snowball saw some papers hanging up in a rack just inside the shop. He tried to get them with his mouth.

The woman laughed.

'No, no, not those! Those aren't the right

ones. Have you come for the papers all by yourself? Wait a minute and I'll get them for you.'

She went inside the shop. Snowball mounted the two steps up to the shop, pushed open the door and walked inside. The woman laughed again as she wrapped up the five papers in brown paper and string.

'I never knew such a pony, never! Coming for the papers on the right day, and walking into my shop, after ringing the bell and all!

You ought to be in a circus!'

Snowball had no money, so he couldn't pay. He took the roll of papers in his mouth and stamped out of the shop. He galloped all the way back to the farm.

He saw Willie's father in the field nearby and ran up to him. He dropped the papers at his feet.

'Bless us all!' cried the farmer, in astonishment and delight. 'Don't tell me you've fetched the papers all by yourself! Snowball, you're a wonder, you really are! Thank you, little pony, you're a good little fellow, and I'll give you four of my best carrots as a reward!'

And he did!

Chapter 11
Snowball at the
Garden Party

One day Mother had a letter and she read it out to the children. 'It's from Lady Tomms,' she said. 'She's going to hold a big garden party in her grounds, and there will be all kinds of side-shows to make money to go towards the hospital.'

'Are we going?' said the children, eagerly.

'Well, Lady Tomms wonders if you would like to organise some races, Willie – and Sheila, she thought perhaps you could make

72

some little flower button-holes and sell them.'

'Mother, I don't want to organise races,' said Willie.

'And when I sold buttonholes before, hardly anyone bought them,' said Sheila.

'Well – I'd like you to do *something* to help!' said Mother.

Timmy had a sudden idea. 'Mother! I know what we could do! We could take Snowball and charge children ten pence a ride!'

'That's a very good idea,' said Mother.

'I could plait a red ribbon in his mane, and brush his tail out beautifully,' said Sheila. 'Oh Mother, wouldn't everyone love Snowball?'

So it was decided that Snowball should be taken along to the garden party, and should give rides to the children there. Mother thought they ought to charge twenty pence, not ten pence.

The children told Dan about it, and he had a fine idea. 'I believe I could make you a little pony-cart, a very small one, just big enough for Snowball to draw,' he said.

Dan kept his word. He made a most beautiful little cart, with two big wheels, which he painted red, with yellow spokes. He painted the cart red too, with a yellow line running round it, and made a set of harness from some old leather straps for Snowball.

'Perhaps Snowball won't like it,' said Sheila. But he did. He felt very grown-up and important to have a cart of his own.

He looked simply lovely trotting along with the little cart behind him. Timmy often rode in it, and he said it was almost as nice as riding on Snowball's back.

The day of the garden party came. Sheila had bought some dark red ribbon, and she carefully plaited it in and out of Snowball's thick black mane. Then she brushed his tail out beautifully.

They put Snowball into the shafts of the little cart that Dan had made, and set off to Lady Tomms' big garden. They found Lady Tomms and she showed them where they were to take children for rides, up and down the big drive.

'How lovely your pony looks!' she said. 'I always do like Shetland ponies, but I think yours is the very nicest that I've ever seen.'

There were all kinds of side-shows and

races and competitions.

But the favourite side-show of all was Snowball!

First Willie called out loudly, 'Rides on Snowball, twenty pence a time! Rides on Snowball, twenty pence a time!'

Then Sheila lined up the children, waiting for their turn. Timmy took their money and put it proudly into a big red bag. Then Willie helped each child on in his turn and took them trotting up and down the drive.

Soon Sheila brought out the red and yellow cart, and Willie called out loudly, 'Rides for the tiny ones, ten pence each. Only ten pence a ride in this lovely little cart!'

Then the very tiny children were lined up with their mothers, waiting their turn. Timmy took their money. Their mothers lifted them into the little cart behind Snowball, and Willie led the pony up and down the drive. The tiny children were delighted.

How hard the three children and Snowball worked all that afternoon! Three times Timmy's bag was full and he had to go to Lady Tomms and empty it. You will never guess how much money he had at the end of the afternoon!

'My dears, do you know you have made twenty-five pounds and ten pence out of pony-rides?' said Lady Tomms, in surprise. 'More than any other side-show has made. It is simply wonderful.'

Willie, Sheila and Timmy were so pleased. Sheila hugged Snowball and whispered into his ear, 'I'm so proud of you, Snowball.'

Wouldn't you love to ride on Snowball? Well, if you ever see a dear little black Shetland pony, call out Snowball! Snowball!

If he comes running to you and nuzzles his nose into your hand, you'll know what he wants to say. 'I like you! You can have a ride on my back!'